Teletubbies™

Little Lamb

SCHOLASTIC INC.
New York Toronto London Auckland Sydney Mexico City New Delhi Hong Kong

One day in Teletubbyland, something appeared from far away.

It was a little lamb.

Oh!
Little lamb!

baa-aa-aa

Laa-Laa thought the little lamb was sad . . .

so Laa-Laa did a little dance to make the little lamb happy.

Laa-laa!

Laa-li-laa!

Laa-li-laa!

Laa-laa li-laa!

But the little lamb was still sad.

baa-aa-aa

Ahhhh!

Along came Tinky Winky.

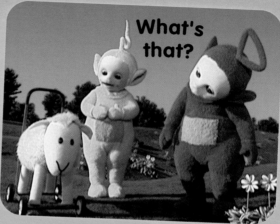

Tinky Winky thought the little lamb was sad because it wanted to be by the flowers.

There.

There!

But the little lamb was **still** sad.

Along came Dipsy.

Dipsy thought the little lamb was sad because it wanted to wear his hat.

Little lamb wear hat!

There.

There!

But the little lamb was **still** sad.

Along came Po.

Po thought the little lamb was sad because it wanted to ride her scooter.

Little lamb ride scooter!

There.  There!

But the little lamb was **still** sad.

baa-aa-aa

Ahhhh!

Then the Teletubbies heard a noise.

baaaaaa

baa-aa-aa

baaaaaa

baa-aa-aa

baaaaaa

baa-aa-aa

baa-aa-aa

baaaa

It was another little lamb!

The little lambs were HAPPY!

Happy lambs!

Teletubbies love each other very much!

Big Hug!

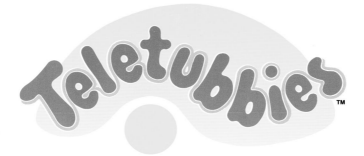

Look for these other Teletubbies storybooks:

ISBN 0-439-10601-X

From the original TV scripts by Andrew Davenport.
Text, design, and illustrations copyright BBC Worldwide.
TELETUBBIES characters and logo: TM and © 1999 Ragdoll Productions (UK) Ltd.
Licensed by The itsy bitsy Entertainment Company. All rights reserved.
Published by Scholastic Inc.
SCHOLASTIC and associated logos are trademarks
and/or registered trademarks of Scholastic Inc.

12 11 10 9 8 7 6 5 4 3 2 1   9/9 0/0 1/0 2/0 3/0

Printed in the U.S.A.

First Scholastic printing, November 1999